A GROWING-UP BOOK™

Every Morning at Play Group

By Michaela Muntean ◆ Illustrated by Tom Cooke

Featuring JIM HENSON'S SESAME STREET MUPPETS

A SESAME STREET / GOLDEN PRESS BOOK

Published by Western Publishing Company, Inc. in conjunction with Children's Television Workshop.

K L M N O P Q R S T

Every morning Emily's mother went to work, Emily's
father went to work, and Emily's brother, Teddy, went
to first grade. And every morning Emily went to Sesame
Street Play Group.

On the first day of play group, Emily's mother and father introduced her to the teacher, Mrs. Brown.

Mrs. Brown showed Emily her own cubby for her jacket. She showed her the shelves filled with picture books and crayons and blocks and balls and trucks.

"This looks like fun," said Emily's mother.

Emily thought so, too.

Then the teacher introduced Emily to Betty Lou and Grover and Max and Big Bird.

"I hope I can remember everybody's name," Emily thought.

When it was time for the grownups to leave, Emily's mother said, "I will be back this afternoon to take you home."

Suddenly Emily felt sad. The afternoon was a long way off!

Her mother gave her an extra-big hug. "If you look out the window when Daddy and I go, we can wave to each other," she told Emily.

So Emily ran to the window and waved good-by. Big Bird waved to his Granny Bird, too.

Mrs. Brown handed Emily a tray of red and blue and
yellow and purple blocks. She gave Big Bird some
paper and a box of crayons. Big Bird and Emily sat on
the floor next to each other. Big Bird drew a picture of
his nest, and Emily built a tall, tall block tower.

Max watched. "I'd like to make a tower, too," he said, and he picked up two blocks from the tray.

"But Mrs. Brown gave them to me!" Emily said.

"They're everyone's blocks," Max said as he bumped Emily's tower. It toppled to the ground.

"He knocked over my tower!" Emily cried.

Mrs. Brown brought over another tray of blocks. "There are enough blocks to share," she said. "Why don't you build a city of towers—together?"

Soon there were block towers and houses and even a bridge! The other children in the play group came over to see the city Max and Emily had built.

Then Mrs. Brown took the children outside to the playground. There was a jungle gym, a see-saw, a sandbox, and two swings. Everyone ran to the swings.

"You'll have to take turns swinging," Mrs. Brown called from the steps.

Betty Lou and Max were the first to swing. When it was Emily's turn, Big Bird pushed her so that she could swing higher.

After lunch and a quiet time for rest, Mrs. Brown handed each child a musical instrument and sat down at the piano. "Now let's play and sing 'Twinkle, Twinkle, Little Star' together," she said.

At first it just sounded like noise. But the second time they played the song they listened to each other, and it sounded like music.

"It's story time!" said Mrs. Brown. "Today it is
Grover's turn to pick a book. Tomorrow you may pick
one, Emily."

Grover chose a story about baby animals. Mrs. Brown
read it to the group and showed the pictures.

Then she said, "Soon it will be time to go home.
Tomorrow please bring a toy or a book or anything
special you'd like to show to the group."

Emily knew just what she wanted to bring.

Soon the parents started to arrive to pick up their children. Emily's mother came to take Emily home. "Good-by!" said Big Bird. "I'll see you tomorrow." Max and Grover and Betty Lou waved good-by, too.

That night at home, everyone in Emily's family talked about the day at work or at school or at play group.

Emily had many new things to talk about. She told about building the block city with Max and swinging in the playground with Big Bird. She told about playing the cymbals at music time, and that it would be her turn to choose a book at story time.

When Daddy tucked Emily in bed she asked, "Am I going to play group again tomorrow?"

"Yes," said Daddy. "You go to play group every morning."

The next morning at breakfast Emily asked, "Could we all stay home together today?"

"No, Emily," said her mother. "On the weekend we'll all do something together. But today we're going to work and school and play group."

"Isn't it your turn to choose the storybook today?" asked her daddy.

"Don't you want to build block towers again with Max?" asked Teddy.

"Yes," said Emily slowly, "and I have something special to take to play group!"

She ran to her room to get it.

Emily held her bunny with the floppy ears very tightly all the way to play group.

"You'll meet my friend Big Bird," she said to Bunny. "And you'll meet Grover and Betty Lou and Max and our teacher, Mrs. Brown. Don't worry. I'll help you remember their names."

"I think you're really going to like play group," she
whispered to Bunny.